To my King all glory.

Dedicated to my wife.

West of Repentance

Zino Paulus

Those who in the day of their peace were proud, and haughty, and terrible, are quite dispirited when trouble comes. Their faces shall be scorched with the flame. All comfort and hope shall fail. The stars of heaven shall not give their light, the sun shall be darkened. Such expressions are often employed by the prophets, to describe the convulsions of governments. God will visit them for their iniquity, particularly the sin of pride, which brings men low. There shall be a general scene of horror. Those who join themselves to Babylon, must expect to share her plagues. All that men have, they would give for their lives, but no man's riches shall be the ransom of his life. Pause here and wonder that men should be thus cruel and inhuman, and see how corrupt the nature of man is become. And that little infants thus suffer, which shows that there is an original guilt, by which life is forfeited as soon as it is begun. The day of the Lord will, indeed, be terrible with wrath and fierce anger, far beyond all here stated. Nor will there be any place for the sinner to flee to, or attempt an escape. But few act as though they believed these things.

- Mathew Henry

Joseph's heart ran like a river. At times gentle, softly familiar, then fathomless and roaring with the rage of swollen waters toward a great wide open. *What is my life overshadowed by fear?* He looked out of the window of his one room apartment onto the road that led through Repentance, a small town somewhere in the Nevadan desert, now covered by night. *Living death*. His view lit by myriad heavenly bodies and a dim streetlight below, he knew, short of forestalling with a bullet, the painfully persistent demand for deliverance within him would be utterly victorious or slowly vanquished.

After some time thus abstracted, he perceived a lone silhouette steal across the pavement. It moved, almost dancingly, as if to avoid apprehension, when the abrupt blare of a distorted loudspeaker harshed the quiet of that midnight hour with the command to stop.

Penetrated to the marrow, the figure stood transfixed into obedience as the unmarked patrol crept up and flooded its intrusive high beam, revealing a petrified boy of no more than seventeen. Breach of curfew. An officer in civilian attire stepped forth and strode toward him with an air of calm delectation. A brief exchange ensued. The kid's cowered posture stood contradistinct to the wide stance of the interrogator, who motioned him to turn and cross his hands behind his back. The cuffs clasped down before he was grasped by the shoulder and shoved against a wall. Joseph mirrored the repulsed bewilderment on the shackled detainee's face as the man stroked his cheek, then, out of nowhere, rammed a fist into the boy's stomach, causing him to collapse and roll up in the dirt. The officer took a handful of the victim's hair and pulled him up to the level of his belt. He looked over his shoulder and called out to his partner. They laughed.

Joseph stumbled backward to his bed, lifted the mattress and retrieved his rifle. His hands trembled as he opened the window. He took aim, chambered a round and attempted to regulate his breath. Still held by the hair, the boy was dragged and thrown into the back of the patrol. Joseph had the officer in his sights when he entered the passenger side. The car soon slid out of range.

Crickets resumed their secret chorus while the false peace of that velvet night swallowed all trace of what had transpired there.

He was only a child when it began. Reports and rumors of people befallen with vicious infection of the psyche started to surface and increase. The code of law implemented in response went back as far as Joseph remembered. A peculiar thing to those present at the outbreak, it soon became commonplace. Over time, no voice divergent from authorized narrative was heard. Such voices were dangerous, as they undermined the best efforts to overcome fearful times. Experts agreed, irrational precepts contained in certain religious expression were detrimental to soundness of mind, heightening the risk of contamination. Houses of worship were shut, solemn assembly outlawed in order to dam virality. To bear arms was furthermore decreed a privilege no longer viable in the hands of citizens liable to lose accountability at any given moment.

Permission to go outside became restricted. Many lost work, depleted savings and went into debt, plunging the town into disrepair, while legends of deranged delinquents and rogue rebels in the surrounding country began to circulate. The merit of such rumors was hard to ascertain, as leaving one's municipality had long become a punishable offense.

Unable to sleep much of the night, Joseph lay in bed 'til near noon before he finally pulled himself up and poured yesterday's coffee.

When he stepped out, temperate morning air gave way to bone dry heat that blurred the sweltered sand all around, save westward, where the frosted peaks of the

Sierra drew his gaze along their ancient profile. He took obscure roads, much deserted, more likely to come across a coyote than another human.

Once he reached the town center a crowd stood gathered before a stage outside the courthouse. *An exemption,* Joseph thought. Such dispensation of public assembly ordinance was frequently granted, contingent somehow on the nature of the occasion. He looked on from across the street as the mayor, a stout, middle aged man by the name of Victor Sothis, took the podium.

“Neighbors, family and friends, welcome! Today we celebrate the sacrifice of those of you who demonstrate personal compromise, crucial for life in our time. You are indeed beacons, everyday heroes by which this, our beloved community, stands or falls. Give yourselves a hand!"

They did.

When the applause faded, the mayor went on, "We must nonetheless urge each and every one of you to yet more vigilance, more decisive action against those who, by their deluded and outdated ideology, would recklessly endanger the rest of us."

More applause followed.

"Some of you have embraced technological progress and taken the Freedom Fraternity Facilitator. You lead your brothers and sisters in humanity by prudent example. Soon the rest, who do not, of their own volition, choose to put social safety above selfish interests, will likewise join us in a better world. Do not get left behind as we, together as one, usher in a brighter future."

They cheered.

"Now, I hope you're all ready for the fabulous, musical sensation, Daphne Donaghue!"

The crowd grew louder.

The object of their admiration was wheeled onto the stage atop a large, golden paper mache bull, scantily clad in purple.

"Give it up for Mayor Sothis!" she encouraged as the blare of the sound system drowned out the audience.

Joseph walked away.

After spending the better part of the day sorting through scrap metal for resale at the junkyard, he bought bread and whiskey with his wages.

“Water of life,” the shopkeeper cracked wise and bagged the bottle.

The sun began to turn red on its descent when he made his way back home. Those destitute enough took up their abode along the sidewalks. The pestilent stench of human waste no longer bothered them, at least not enough to settle elsewhere. A frail woman stood leaned against a deserted building.

“Need love?” she asked.

Of course, Joseph thought and kept on.

Her lewd male counterpart stepped out of the shadows. “Maybe *I’m* more up his alley.”

“Or he just thinks he’s better than us,” she yelled.

Passing the windowfront of a dive, Joseph spotted an acquaintance from his early school days by the bar. He’d looked forward to bolting the door behind him for the night, even still, the sight of a face faintly familiar from pleasant obscurity compelled him to stop for a moment. Just then the fellow turned, recognized and began to wave him over with some enthusiasm. Ousted from solitary contemplation, Joseph walked over and stepped across the threshold. If most small businesses had taken a hit to the point of collapse, this wasn’t one of them.

Names and recollections from a shared, albeit removed past gave cause for laughter and reminiscence until, a handful of rounds later, topics of discussion gained ostensible depth.

“Right and wrong isn’t a question of opinion,” Joseph asserted. “The inherent order in all things is self evident.”

The fellow shook his head. “It’s only ever a question of perspective.”

“Surely there’s things you would condemn as fundamentally bad, regardless of whether a given society has come to condone them or not.”

“Your idea of morality is instilled into you by your surroundings. Reality in and of itself makes no such judgments.”

Joseph's initial cheerfulness gave way to a more familiar, loathsome sensation. The doctrine further espoused by his former schoolmate culminated in a do what thou wilt attitude, its adherents unburdened of any binding principle based on objective distinction between good and evil. All of it struck Joseph as the latter. Although his instinctive conviction never wavered, he had to begrudgingly admit to himself that he possessed no definitive argument against such abhorrent claims.

It went on for some time. Exhausted, public curfew finally gave him the excuse to part ways, dissatisfied, if not disgusted at having shaken hands.

Back in his room he sat by the window and twisted open the whiskey. The bottle was near empty when the daystar's colossal reach began to dye the world in color once more.

Your life wastes away, yet you do nothing. The yawning weight of your nothingness in turn fixes you in place. Perpetual paralysis. All you do is pass the buck. To waste the life you're given, that's the gravest offense. Each day comes with promise of the new and passes as no more than a phantom of the last. Again and again and again. Endlessly. But you just watch, watch and lament yourself quietly. Coward. Why don't you do something? You'd rather permit yourself lofty thoughts. You think you're better than others. How could a man do anything when he doesn't know who he is? You can't call that a man. Who are you? The words you say, every pathetic gesture, an empty mask behind which you hide, only you don't know who or what you're hiding. Your masquerade harbors ill, to befall you and those around you like some accursed, self fulfilling prophecy. You nurse your self pity in the void of your defiled soul and so you've become a thing weak and ugly. Vicious. Dishonorable… I can't feel anymore. I reach but I can't grasp. There is no anchor. I'm floating away. I'm a shadow. I don't know who I am.

The rifle under his mattress flashed through his fevered mind. His translucent silhouette in the window seemed to fade against the boundless desert sky as he passed out into reduced consciousness.

Joseph's skull roared when he went to pick up groceries for his grandfather.

The old man lived in a house on a patch of land by the edge of town. He'd built the place for his wife on the soil he bought as a young man. His proudest memory always had been the look on her face when he first showed it to her. A fearsome reputation stuck ever since he shot at a banker who came to buy the place out from under him due to rumors of a coal deposit beneath the ground. People remembered. They generally kept away.

Joseph was greeted by the small terrier he'd known since he was a boy. The only thing different about the animal was its mustache, which had gotten more prominent and gray over time. Its vigor remained unchanged. "Good boy."

He knocked on the screen door. “Herman, you there?” Pushing it open, he stepped in and sorted the food into the cabinets in the kitchen. The buzzing fridge was empty except for a pack of beers. He took out a crisp can, held it to his forehead, cracked it open and downed it, followed by a deep belch that made the dog start up.

“That’s... better.” Joseph grabbed two more and went outback.

Herman was busy with the drill in his workshop, unable to hear him approach over the machine’s penetrant noise.

“Heckfire!” the old man exclaimed when he saw his grandson suddenly standing there. “You scared the stones off me boy.” He cut the power, took off his gloves and went to greet Joseph with a brief embrace. “No need to finish me now, time’ll do the job soon enough.”

“You okay?” Joseph asked.

Herman ignored the question. “Did you get the peppered beef?”

“Jup,” Joseph affirmed with some satisfaction.

Fresh meat wasn’t always so simple to come by anymore. You had to know a guy who knew a guy if you wanted more than the sanctioned allotment and preferred to abstain from officially endorsed protein source alternatives, such as rodents and roaches.

He sat on the edge of a table and tossed Herman a beer. The red and gold marine corps banner hung up on the wall had always fascinated him. His grandpa was the reason Joseph had kept his rifle, never registered nor dropped it off to be melted down like the law required.

"What're you workin' on?" he asked.

"The bomb."

Joseph snickered but probably wouldn't have put it past him. "Are you doing something for Remembrance Day with the guys this year?"

"Most of them can't even remember to wipe themselves anymore. It ain't much of a get together." Herman took a draft from his beer.

"You still think back on those times?"

"Once in a while."

"Ever miss it?"

"I fought men who didn't provoke me on land that wasn't mine for people I never met. I thought I was honor bound."

"You were."

The old man adjusted the gauge on his drill. "It didn't take long to see the foul fruit honor bears when turned on its head by those who have none. Believing the enemy to be across the shores was our gravest defeat."

"You did what you thought was right. At least you did *something*."

"Take a look around you son. Where the blind lead the blind, both fall into a pit." He turned his attention back to his work until he stopped the machine and spoke up again, “Have you thought about going to church assembly? Pastor Moser asked about you.”

“My mind’s been all over the place.”

“You ought to go.”

Joseph crushed his empty can and tossed it into the trash in the corner.

A small congregation sat gathered in the basement of Pastor John Moser’s home the following Saturday night. Lights outside sparsely penetrated the narrow frosted glass window by the ceiling as his calm, steady inflection permeated the room.

“Be strong in the Lord, and in the power of his might. Put on the whole armour of God, that ye may be able to stand against the wiles of the devil. For we wrestle not against flesh and blood, but against principalities, against powers, against the rulers of the darkness of this world, against spiritual wickedness in high places.”

He looked up from the Book.

“We see those unguided by the Word of their Creator, our very neighbors, led astray into the dark, bound in hopeless confusion. Many sense doom, yet for the life of them remain unable to tell left from right, void of light. Some think themselves neutral, in a world where neutrality always sides with wickedness. Worse still weighs the deception of those who, deluded into prideful oblivion, actually believe themselves on the right side of history, in fulfillment of mankind's inevitable, triumphant march toward humanist utopia, until they once more, yet again, in one final pandemonic cataclysm, find themselves engulfed by mass graves, the depth and width of which cast their souls into eternal perplexity. All these, enamored with sin, are ensnared by them who *do* have insight, *do* remain in control of their faculty, purposefully electing to lay it at the altar of the adversary. In those is neither benevolence to be sought, nor mercy to be found. So where does that leave us, where do we stand?" He pointed toward a wooden cross fixed upon the wall. "The answer is given to us in the eternal voice of our King. We stand firm upon the rock of His Word, against which the tides of this world must crash and be broken on the day of reckoning."

What followed was a thorough and in depth verse by verse exposition of Scripture. When the sermon concluded they prayed and partook of bread and wine. Afterward, they moved the rug, lifted the floorboards and hid the Bible thereunder.

Joseph had kept to himself with the quiet reticence of a guest. Besides Herman, Aaron, a young man of his own age, was the only one he had a personal connection with. They had been good, at times even best of friends growing up, until their paths separated along the way. It was him who spoke when Joseph took heart and joined a group of conversing believers.

“From what I hear, Freedom Fraternity Facilitator legislation will be passed soon. That’s a line in the sand we can’t cross.”

"We're all in agreement," another replied, "but let's not be naive about the force they'll apply."

They looked to Moser, who stopped in reflection before he responded to their silent appeal, "Punishment for leaving town is draconian. Remove yourself without permission and the weight of the law is visited upon those you leave behind. Therefore I don't make this suggestion lightly." He paused. "It's been about ten years since brother Manasseh quit Repentance for the outer territories."

The name brought a young man to Joseph's recollection who had always seemed larger than life to him. Not yet old enough to make sense of things back then, he'd overheard how Manasseh's fiancé allegedly killed herself after she was seized and committed to a psychiatric sanitorium. Although Joseph's parents never went to church, the man had become a frequent presence in their home for a while, when they first engaged in resistance. Manasseh had narrowly escaped arrest and fled, around the same time Joseph's father and mother were taken away.

"Wherever he is, he may know a way forward," Moser went on. "One of us ought to seek him out."

None came forward.

"I would go myself," he added. "I only hesitate for the same reason as those of you who have wives and children that depend on them. God forbid they should fall into the hands of the investigators on our account."

The men nodded in agreement.

“It will have to be someone who has no family of their own.”

No one there implied or suggested it, but Joseph felt as if those words were meant for him. The image of his grandfather alone on his land came to the fore of his mind.

A fog of repetition shrouded the weeks. Joseph kept himself occupied at the junkyard. At it by sunrise, the hours passed by as the great fiery disk began to beat down on the scrap metal and scorched it to the touch.

Time... Joseph thought and wiped the sweat from his face. It seemed to slip away there. He glanced up at the cloudless blue. If he'd had a sense of promise as a boy, of some glorious fate edged forth from behind the horizon of his life, he didn't see it now. The value of work wasn't lost on him, still, to shift those parts from one stack to the other somehow felt like it just might leave him wasted away. Buried beneath the heap. As each hour, each minute and each second crept along, it was as though he began to run out of oxygen.

The owner of the place strolled up in an oil smeared undershirt, itching the bottom of his vastly protrudent midsection. "You go ahead and call it a day." He nodded toward the exit of the place and shoved a big dip of chewing tobacco into the side of his mouth.

“I’m not near done here, sir,” Joseph replied.

“Well, you’re as done as you’re gonna be. The people meant to pick that up canceled, which means I can’t pay you ‘til either them, or someone else, pays *me*.”

“Sir, all due respect, I need my wages. At least in part.”

He looked at Joseph and spat brown slosh into the sand. “Respect has nothing to do with it. You don’t get paid ‘til I do. Now vacate my property.” At that, he turned away and walked back toward his box of an office.

Joseph felt his pulse shoot up with indignation. He glanced down at a fist sized rock by his feet with a mind to nail the transgressor in the back of his shiny dome, just before the man slammed the screen door shut behind himself.

The day still ablaze with heat, he went into the corner store.

“That’d be all?” the clerk asked and bagged the whiskey.

Handing him the last of his money, Joseph went home to nurse the bottle until night fell with him into uneasy sleep.

Herman’s voice broke through the silence, dawn yet concealed beyond the horizon.

Joseph leaned over to the window and saw the man beneath the faint orb of night with his arms raised toward him, his fishing cap on and a thermos of coffee in his hand.

“Give me a minute.” He rubbed his face and yawned. He’d forgotten their trip.

“What’s that?”

“I’ll be right down.”

“Alrighty then!” Herman exclaimed as if to himself and strutted over to his truck.

The stream which flowed down into Repentance from high up in the Sierra was interwoven with the fabric of Joseph's memory as with the land itself.

White and blue oaks thickened along the banks as the two men followed a dirt road and crossed the edge of town where constellations shone with a moist glare against the obsidian firmament. The scent of the woods, carried by the night's breeze, entered through the open windows and quickened their senses.

They had reached a calm bend in the creek and set up their gear when day began to break in an aurora of fiery maroon. By the time they reclined in their camping chairs, baited hooks bobbing in the current, a high blue sky had erased all trace of the mystic dark.

"There's a fine line between a fisherman and a fool attached to a pole," Herman remarked.

"A tough one for the straddling."

The old man cracked a slight smile at the quip.

Joseph spun his reel and watched the sinker skip over the surface. "The thought of coming up empty… the fool with no catch to show for… it's scary sometimes."

"The whole world is filled with people who're more or less scared. Truth alone breaks the yoke of fear."

"Mom and dad fought for truth. So much for that..."

"I often tried to convince those two, there's nothing worthwhile without the Creator it emanates from. I failed in that," Herman said.

“Why would God make people that go astray from Him? Why does He allow evil and pain if He *is* the Creator, in control of everything?”

“There’s no love apart from free will. Likewise, there’s no love in disallowing someone to exist because you know they’ll be flawed or even turn away from you. That means since God’s defining attribute *is* love, it was in accordance with His nature to create people, and to create them with the choice to embrace or reject Him. Without it, we would be no more than meat puppets. No loving relationship could exist. We’re made in His image, which means with intellect, self determination and responsibility, not as mindless slaves. Besides, the clay doesn’t get to reprimand the potter.”

They sat in silence for some time.

Herman replaced the bait on his hook, which had been chewed off. Spud rested in the shade of his master's legs and only tilted an ear in the direction of sounds registered once in a while. Uninterrupted, the steady rush of water became almost meditative. Prayerful. Like some substance of purity issued forth infinitely.

“I remember the last night I saw them,” Joseph recalled. “Mom tucked me into bed. Dad came in after her to kiss me goodnight, like he always did.” The image came to life in the mirror of his mind. “That spicy pipe tobacco smell on his shirt... he spoke about integrity, righteousness. There was a difference though… a different tone. I couldn’t put my finger on it, but I heard it.” Joseph paused. “I watched him walk out the door. That night in my dream they both fell into bottomless darkness.”

Herman kept his gaze fixed on the stream. "I'm sorry, kid."

Something heavy tugged on Joseph's line.

A massive granite slab was erected in the town center that month. Engraved upon it stood declared the essential tenets of a new age, a novel decalogue, ushered forth as though in salvific response to universal calamity.

It was announced that people would be required by law to touch their foreheads to the manmade monolith when they passed it, as a token of acquiescence to the greater benefit.

Meanwhile summer kicked into high gear. The dog days passed in a haze of heat, like some pyretic mirage on a dried up oasis. Dust permeated the air.

Joseph spent most of his time in his room, where the rusted fan buzzed and cooled him just enough. Sitting on his bed, leaned against the wall, thought swayed into the distant. He daydreamt of a flood. The wet came down without cease, until Repentance lay deluged, its inhabitants made ghosts on sunken burial grounds beneath a wrathful new ocean. Finally his own lungs, filled with sacred rain, ceased their function as the flesh surrendered to this conclusive crescendo of fate. Then the landline rang.

"Hello?"

"Is this Herman's boy?" the woman on the other end asked.

"Yeah," he answered. "Who's asking?"

"This is Janice... Herman's neighbor. I found this number on his fridge."

"What's this about?"

"I'm afraid there's bad news… He had… it appears he's had some kind of a stroke. I, I think that's what it was. We found him in his driveway. He's laid up in bed now, poor thing, but he refuses to be taken to hospital…"

The old man could barely move to acknowledge his grandson's presence. Spud wouldn't stir from his side and only wagged his tail slightly. Joseph's knees weakened when he saw him down like this. He pulled up a chair and remained silent for some time.

"You keep staring at me I might charge a silver dollar," Herman said out of the corner of his mouth, the muscles in one half of his face froze stiff.

"Sorry."

"Well, who can blame you. Not every day you get front row to the freakshow." He pointed at the television with the arm he was able to move. "Throw on one of them good oaters, will ya?"

Joseph obliged. Then he laid a blanket over Herman's legs and sat down by his side again.

To upkeep the property and monitor his grandfather's condition were Joseph's main concerns in the time that followed.

One late afternoon as they sat on the porch, he felt the moment right to ask. "Did you take your meds leading up to… up to what happened?"

"Ran out a while back," Herman replied laconically.

"Why didn't you let me know? I could have gone to get more." Joseph was notably upset at the nonchalance.

“Since Richards had his license revoked, he’s been replaced by some goofball. Don’t trust him. Not going back there.”

“Like I said, I’ll go.”

When he entered the doctor's office the neon light made him squint. The sting of sanitizer filled the room to the point that he could almost taste it.

Hammering away on a computer keyboard, a wiry receptionist acknowledged his presence with a short look, the buzz of the lamp above her head interrupted for a split second when a fly drawn into it smoldered away with a sizzling pop.

"I'm here to renew my grandfather's prescription."

She promptly dropped a clipboard with some forms onto the counter. "Fill these out and take a seat. Doctor Ketzler will be with you shortly."

There were magazines laid out on a table. 'Global Health Weekly' featured an article titled 'Protecting Yourself From Others By Protecting Others From Yourself', while some kind of tabloid rag had Daphne Donaghue on the cover. Juice from a glossy apple spilled down her chin with a black eyed albino python draped across her shoulders. The headline was kept in red. 'Who Needs Adam? Time To Get With The Times.'

Joseph's gaze trailed out of the window

toward the Sierra Nevada when he was called.

"What can I do you for?" Ketzler asked.

"I'm here for my grandfather's heart medication." He handed him the script.

The doctor looked it over. "I'm afraid we can't give that out anymore."

"Can't give it out?"

"New regulations. Seniors are temporarily restricted to general preventative measures."

"My grandpa's risk for stroke increases drastically without it. He barely survived the last one."

“I’m sorry, but it is regulation. My hands are tied.”

“So what are we supposed to do?” Joseph was quite unable to conceal the repulsion written on his face.

In turn, the veneer of sympathy vanished from the man’s expression. “Actually, when *was* the last time he received the prescribed dose of general preventative measures?”

“If you withhold his medication the consequences will be on your hands.”

“You seem agitated,” the doctor noted. “Temper is a common symptom... have you been tested recently? The best thing to ensure your grandpappy's health could very well be to isolate you for a spell.”

Looking straight into the spectacled eyes which now glared at him with aloof gratification, Joseph got up.

The receptionist watched him leave with a monotone “stay healthy.”

Back at Herman’s bedside, Joseph told him he’d been unable to obtain it.

“No matter,” the old man asserted. “There’s nothing left keeping me on this earth.” He turned his eyes to Joseph. “Almost nothing.”

The silence between the two men, usually a mutual source of familiar comfort, was suddenly weighed down with inescapable apprehension.

“Why are you still here?” Herman asked.

“I’ve got nowhere to be today…”

“In this hellhole of a town. You don’t believe this is all that’s in store for you, do you?”

Joseph cleared his throat. “I wasn’t going to leave you by yourself.”

“So much for that.”

They both understood his condition would decline fast. Herman reached over to the nightstand beside his bed, rummaged around in the drawer and produced a small Bible. He waved Joseph closer and laid it in his grandson’s hands.

“Listen to me. There are things that happen which we can’t make sense of while we're here. We just can't. But, in Him, we can live a life of truth, in dignity and purpose, regardless of what goes on in this world." He paused. "When you go to serve the Lord, prepare to be put to the test. Set your heart right, keep straight and calm in time of trouble. Stay with Him, never abandon Him, and you will prosper in the end. Accept whatever happens with patience. Gold is tested in fire, a man's character forged in the furnace of affliction."

It was a few weeks later Herman passed on. Unwilling to have the coroner pick up his earthly remains for mandatory cremation, Joseph called Aaron instead.

They dug a grave atop the highest hill on his land, buried him there and planted a Sycamore at the site, watched over until the end of time by the mountains to the west, like a row of colossal guardians in peaceful salutation.

Pastor Moser and his young son William stood in the middle of a cluster of onlookers in the town center, with the perimeter secured by a handful of uniformed men. They were being detained after Moser had failed to touch his forehead to the newly erected standing stone.

“Is this the contempt you have for your fellow citizens?” the lawman asked.

“We meant no harm officer.”

“The harm you meant is plain for all to see. Refusal to subordinate yourself to the greater good.” He scrutinized him. “I know you… you used to be some kind of preacher, right?”

“Yes, sir.”

“Is this your boy?” The officer pointed at William.

“He is.”

“Endangering your own child with your careless conduct...” Looking around at the bystanders, the man raised his voice. “You spouted fairy tales for a living, so now you're going to tell your son that everything you professed was a lie."

Moser kept silent.

"Refusal will be considered proof of instability. I'll have to turn you in for medical examination. Now do it," he demanded. "In front of all these good people you have so blatantly shown your disregard for."

The spectators began to murmur amongst themselves.

"I cannot do what you ask."

"You're gonna have to."

"I cannot."

His displeasure at Moser's collected

countenance increased perceptibly. “You will. Or you’ll be committed for treatment.”

At this, the pastor addressed the crowd, “What will it profit a man to gain the world and lose his own soul? God has extended His merciful hand through His own Son. Take it, while there’s still time! If any one of you would be saved unto eternal life, heed His call now!”

Only shouts of ridicule, insults and threats were hurled his way as he was handcuffed and dragged off.

William grabbed ahold of his coat. “Let my father go!” he screamed.

“Your Father is above.” Moser looked towards heaven. “Call on *Him*.”

When the church convened in their plight once news of their shepherd's arrest had reached them, Joseph announced he would leave town to find Manasseh.

The congregation prayed over him.

That night past curfew he strapped his rifle on his back and pulled Herman's old motorcycle out of the workshop. He filled the tank with gas from dusty canisters stored around the place and fired it up.

The mild evening air streamed across his arms and face as the bike whirred and weaved its way through the streets. So close to the border of town he was almost sure of sweet getaway relief, an undercover patrol spotted and fixed the floodlight on him. He sped up as the megaphone prompted him to halt.

As good as vanished from his pursuers' grasp, the report of a shot cracked bullwhip like through the desert air. Joseph felt a sharp bite in his back. He twisted the throttle to its limit and flew out of Repentance.

The cadenced tremor of the engine and the salient scent of benzene began to merge with the heat of the stars. He didn't know how long it had been when he became aware of the sanguine wet running down his side. As though pulled forward through a tunnel, he rode hard beneath the immense silvery river that ran across the firmament. Then all went black. The bike skidded out beneath him and hurled his limp body into a violent fall somewhere in those barren badlands.

The noonday blaze of a scathing sun burned his skin when he regained consciousness. Blood from his bullet wound had seeped into the sand around him and clotted into thick red clay. His mouth was bone dry. His lips cracked. Desperately parched, water was the only thought.

Joseph groaned as he turned his neck, when, blurred against the horizon there appeared a strange shape, like some gradually manifested specter, until it finally took on the likeness of a rusty old truck. He looked for the weapon, which had been flung a few feet from the wreck.

Approaching fast, he made out several men standing atop the flatbed with long black hair and bizarre masks of black and white corpse paint on their faces. Rez metal blasted from the cabin's open windows, a deep growl of words in some ancient indigenous tongue. Certain he was about to be mercilessly crushed, he braced himself as the truck slid to a halt only inches from his limp body.

They hopped off and proceeded to assess him. When they found him apparently unable to move, they turned their attention to his belongings. One of them picked up the rifle and inspected the action. Another stood up the motorcycle and mounted it. A third rooted through the saddlebags that had fallen off the bike, tossed the Bible into the dust and pocketed a knife and a compass.

Against Joseph's better judgment, he summoned all the strength left in his bloodied limbs and managed to crawl over to the one that held his gun. He grabbed the thief's leg and ripped it out from beneath him. The man crashed onto his back. It wasn't long before he had positioned himself above Joseph and punched down hard onto his face with a thump.

Having gathered anything of value, they appeared set to depart and give the stranger over to the elements and certain demise, when a disagreement erupted amongst them. One young man seemed opposed to the ruthless act of cruelty.

On the verge of oblivion, Joseph felt a low rumble, a tremble in the ground beneath him. There was a thin crackle in his ears. He looked up, slowly raised his arm and pointed toward the sky, across which, in sudden display of celestial magnitude, three gigantic fiery bolides tore their path across the atmosphere in the broad light of that midday hour, dragging their colossal tails like some heavenly triune chariot of war.

“The stars...” Joseph uttered, “they’re falling.”

Now they all looked up.

There was reverent silence until the magnificent astronomical anomaly eventually passed out of view beyond the edge of the earth.

Once they slowly returned to cognizance of the matter at hand, notably affected, even perturbed, the mood had shifted. Rather than deserted, Joseph was loaded onto the truck, tied and blindfolded.

Obscure roads led through deep canyons until they'd reached far into the reservation. After his eyes had adjusted to the harsh light, he found himself on an impoverished rancheria. It was overlooked by a massive cliffside with dozens of small caves strewn across the face of the rock, connected by intricate stairways, hewn with ingenuity that gave record of skill possessed millennia ago. At its foot, a handful of unkempt children chased a crippled old mutt around. Its desperate snarls and snaps, ridiculed with careless laughter, trailed off between decrepit shacks, erected and neglected in stark contrast to the ancient monumental backdrop. A passed out drunk lay slumped over an empty bottle in the dust.

He was taken into the only brick building there and presented to an elderly man.

Unlike the fierce appearance of the raiders, this fellow looked like a regular rancher, except for his long jet black hair, which he had in common with the others.

The one who'd argued for Joseph to be spared spoke into the man's ear and relayed what had occurred before they turned their attention back to him.

"You'll be our guest here," the elder spoke up. "My name is Winston Alo." He looked over. "This is Maddox, my nephew."

"Mad for short," the younger added.

Joseph's injuries were tended by the rancher's old wife. The bullet had gone straight through and exited cleanly without puncturing any organs. Heavy abrasions were all he'd sustained from the crash. When the wound had been cleaned and bound, a strong herbal brew numbed the pain and caused profound sleep.

Once he was well enough, he helped plan and build an irrigation system similar to one he'd constructed with Herman a few years prior to the end of his life.

Maddox and Joseph would work together during the days. The others at least tolerated him, although they mostly kept their distance, with what could have been read as almost superstitious hesitancy. When they weren't out on the reservation, the raiders punished their amplified instruments to maximum capacity, tranced in dark soundscapes that haunted those dry places like some incoherent diabolical outcry. None of the disturbed residents were inclined to voice displeasure. They probably felt it best for the young men to unleash the brunt of their teeming primordial impulse this way as opposed to out there, involved in whatever it was they did.

Maddox related how the people suffered in both spiritual as well as physical poverty. Illness and addiction ran rampant, violence and abuse were commonplace. Joseph noted how things were essentially the same where he came from.

“Your God’s forbidden Book, it’s meant to have answers, right?” Mad asked as they dug channels for drip lines.

"I wouldn't know."

"Might be worth looking into, don't you think?"

Joseph paused and rested on his shovel for a moment. "I guess so. My grandfather used to tell me about prophecies fulfilled throughout history, hundreds of them. He said that's one way God's Word delivers eternal proof of its validity within its own pages."

"I see..."

It began to cool down in the afternoon. The work kept Joseph's mind still, a welcome refuge from the gravity of his circumstance, interrupted when Maddox picked the conversation back up.

"So, who did that to you?" He gestured toward the injury.

"I broke curfew. When they saw me head out of town they followed and shot me."

"Land of the free… what now?"

His inquiry forced Joseph to consider. The people back in Repentance were counting on him, for what exactly he did not know. In any case, it was time to push on. He explained that he'd been sent to look for Manasseh, who had left some years ago and was rumored to be up in the mountains somewhere.

To Joseph's surprise, Mad told him that if this Manasseh was the one he thought, he and his gang, the infamous Range of Light Rebels, were known to run guns and intercept government transports.

"There's a supply truck that should be coming over on Route 50 in a few days. That's their turf. If you're lucky you might catch them trying to catch it."

They rode in silence for some time. The rumble of Mad's truck was the only sound set against the quiet of the stone faced valley they followed. Spared the blindfold, Joseph observed the environment, bare and parched by merciless heat, habitation to strange beasts, all adapted to the severe.

A rusty *U.S. Route 50* sign with probably as many bullet holes in it marked the desert highway. '*Welcome to the loneliest road in America*.' The faded slogan read like a surreal glimpse into a different time.

They stopped and got out.

The open road reached beyond the blurred horizon, melted against the arid air like landscapes painted on heated wax. Mad walked around the truck and took Joseph's saddlebags and rifle from the bed. He lowered the ramp to let down the motorcycle.

"You hold on to it," Joseph decided. "I'd better stay out of sight and keep to the rocks. Besides, I'd run outta gas anyways."

"You sure?"

"It belonged to a special man. Take care of it."

Maddox affirmed with a smile on his face. "They have to pass the crossroad, should be here sometime before midnight." He pointed out the direction. "Oh, almost forgot..." Pulling Joseph's Bible from his pocket, he brushed it off and handed it to its owner.

"Where'd you get this?" Joseph burst out. "I thought I'd lost it!"

"Picked it up the day we found you. I took the liberty to look through it..." He paused. "Keep your guard up." His suddenly casual manner masked concern for the uncertain path which lay before his newfound friend.

"I will. Thank you."

Joseph watched him disappear the way they'd come in a cloud of dust.

He walked until he eventually reached the crossing, where he hid himself between two large boulders by the side of the road. Nothing or no one could be seen to stir as far as the eye went, except for a fiercely horned, sand colored sidewinder that rushed across the smoldered ground in crafty contortion. When dusk fell Sirius rose against the horizon as Orion turned and glistened overhead.

Night far spent, the highway remained dead. Doubtful and weary of waiting, Joseph finally decided to return to the reservation.

He'd gone about a mile before shots cracked in the distance behind him. By the time he doubled back a scene of chaos had unfolded beneath the moon's icy gleam.

A midsized transporter lay turned on its side in the ditch, one front wheel spinning slowly while its harsh headlights pierced the dark. The uniformed driver had crashed through the windshield and come to a halt a few feet further, in bizarre display of mortal fragility, hurled into eternity in the duration of a moment. A pickup was stopped lengthwise in the middle of the road. In front of it lay another man, this one in plain clothes, perhaps one of the outlaws, shot to pieces, bleeding out on the concrete.

Joseph let the bags drop to the ground and swung the rifle from his shoulder. He saw the back of another transport guard standing over what appeared to be a second bandit, forced to his knees, pistol pointed at his skull. There was a heated exchange of words between them.

“This is it…” Joseph whispered. He knew if he failed to act now, he would miss what might be his only chance to find Manasseh. Taking a deep breath, he stepped out from behind the rocks and slowly edged his way forward. The one on his knees spotted Joseph. He quickly averted his gaze to distract the would be executioner as he continued the effort to talk himself out of a bullet in the head.

When the guard heard the footsteps behind him and turned around, he received the butt of Joseph’s rifle to the forehead and collapsed like a sack of stones.

The outlaw now rose to his feet, picked up the gun and in turn pointed it at the unconscious man with what looked like lethal intent.

"He's no threat," Joseph interceded.

"This bastard killed my friend."

Joseph looked over at the dead transport driver. "Seems you're even."

Finally, the man shoved the pistol into his belt. "Where'd you come from and why'd you do this?"

"I was told you might help me."

"Help you how?"

"I'm looking for Manasseh. We're from the same town, I came to find him."

The man appeared to contemplate for a moment. He glanced around as if to make sure Joseph was alone. "Well, it appears I owe you… Ike's the name."

Supplies from the transport together with the dead outlaw's body were heaved onto the pickup.

Once at the base of the mountains, they rode up the steady incline, so that by the time they arrived morning had broken.

The camp was buried in the backwoods high up in the Sierra. It consisted of a logwood house in the middle of a clearing, surrounded by trailers, campers and trucks.

"Wait here," Ike prompted, got out and disappeared into the building.

The scenery had gone from the barren wilderness below, with its age old rock formations set against the sweeping sky, to the lush shelter of alpine woods, all shades of green abuzz with birdsong.

After a while, Ike reappeared in the door and waved him over. “Watch your step!” he called.

Joseph passed a deep black pit, left from what appeared to be an old well in the ground. He glanced down into it for a moment and walked toward the house, where he was disarmed and patted down.

Manasseh sat at a roundtable with a handful of others. There were maps and a few pistols spread out before them. The man's countenance, in essence like to Joseph’s faint recollection, bore the indelible gravity of toilful tribulation. He must have been in his early thirties now, strains of white already lining his full beard and shoulder length hair. His presence gave witness to one who, by prowess, predestination or whatever other power, had proceeded from the impotent realm of passivity to the potency of willful existence. He appeared as a man in bold transcendence of some kind of unspoken line in the sand, at herculean peace with his Damoclean bargain.

The reverence evident in those around him was that paid by warriors to a commander who went ahead of them into the thickest action, willed to stand or fall as they did.

His cloudless eyes pierced the new arrival as he leaned back into his heavy mahogany chair. “Young Ike here says he might not be among the living if it weren’t for you.”

Joseph hesitated. “I just happened to be in the right place at the right time.”

“Just happened to be...”

“I set out to find you,” he conceded.

“Well... here I am.” Manasseh threw up his hands in an open gesture. “Now what?”

One of the men at the table, a hard faced roughneck with foul teeth and slicked back hair, hissed as if to himself, “I say he’s a snake.”

Joseph noticed and so did the others. He held his peace as best he could when the room was suddenly weighed down.

Finally, the fellow lost restraint and looked straight at him. “Seems like much too much of a happy coincidence to me. I say you're a snake."

Manasseh watched in silence, as if to observe a new turn revealed in some stage play.

"I heard you the first time," Joseph answered.

"So what're you gonna do about it, snake?" The man thrust his chair back with a screech and stood up. He walked over until there was only about an inch left between them.

Ike tried to step in. "Draven, he saved my hide out there."

"You stay out of this."

Draven pushed Joseph.

"Don't do it again."

He shoved him a second time without hesitation, when Joseph anticipated his movement, swung and landed a punch flush on his jaw. The impact rocked Draven and caused him to stumble back. Stunned, he held the side of his chin.

"You messed up now..." he lunged forward.

They fell to the ground, where an intense grapple ensued. It took all of Joseph's strength to control his assailant, until he finally managed to roll over and put him in a choke. "Are you done?" Joseph yelled, his rage now untethered and channeled into the pressure which he brought to bear upon his opponent's neck. He repeated his question and applied even more force, "Are you done?"

Unable to answer, the man grunted and choked. When Joseph saw concession of defeat he got off him.

“If I’m to leave, you may as well kill me. I have nothing to go back to.”

Now Manasseh rose to his feet. “That’ll do.” He signaled for Draven to back away. “What’s your name kid and where’d you come from?”

“We’re from the same town. I’m Caleb and Amelia’s son, Joseph. Pastor Moser and the others sent me to find you.”

Months flew by. The Range of Light Rebels, known so among friend and foe, took their appellation from the upland terrain they held sway over. When they weren't engaged in the acquisition of arms and munitions for redistribution to the highest bidder, they systematically liberated government property, all kinds of goods in raid after raid, heist after heist. Where the roads ran through mountain passes, they lay in ambush. When transports came, depredation commenced. Reckless of their lives, they rose up against a world that would crush them under its heel, knowing if they returned to their hometowns, they'd be incarcerated or worse. Hunted outlaws, they neither expected nor gave quarter. In their estimation, all opposed to the natural rights inherent to free men utterly forfeited the sanctuary thereof.

The charismatic captain gave meaning to the phrase chivalry of crime, as part of the plunder was used to relieve the distressed, the destitute and dispossessed from surrounding areas. This went some way toward a certain perception of the band. Meanwhile the reality of those caught in lethal crossfire was accepted as remorsefully inevitable.

Manasseh had affirmed they would find a solution to help the folks back in Repentance once they'd consolidated their present circumstance. As time passed, the radical rush of outlaw life became irresistible intoxication to Joseph. Utterly contradistinct to that old, stifling numbness burrowed into subconscious depth, he found himself swept up by this, the carefree hazard of unrestrained life.

It had been almost a year when Joseph and Ike, returning from one of their frequent hunting expeditions, navigated the pine edged glades of the range, unstirred beneath immaculate skies, the weight of the buck they'd harvested on their shoulders.

Back at the main house, they learned of a handful of families who had fled persecution and, in need of shelter, were brought to camp. Among these was a young woman.

Miriam was different from the girls one might have encountered in town. She carried herself with none of the harsh undertone common to her peers, which gave witness to a hardened, triumphal depravity. Instead, a dignified kindness went out from her.

The first time they talked was in the midst of a blustery summer storm, brought under the roof of the same wooden shack by gusts of rain that whipped down onto the rocks outside. They had related to each other with a sense of mindful measure, even veneration. A mutual sympathy, visited upon them before the first word was ever uttered, reached effortlessly beyond the mundane. By the time the storm subsided, burning white stars lit the satin black canopy. They walked in the petrichor perfume of the freshly soaked earth and parted, both eager for their next encounter with an innocent, unspoken elation. *She is beautiful...* Joseph thought.

Tipped off about a rival outfit's unguarded armory ripe for the picking, the rebels left camp before sunup.

What was supposed to be an easy take turned carnage as an ambuscade drew shut and left them to fend in led hail, the likes of which even the seasoned veterans in their ranks hadn't seen.

The whizz and whirr of projectiles sliced the air in surreal proximity to their heads, drowned out only by thunderous reports of barrels trained on them from sides two. Pungent odor of nitroglycerin and burnt powder hung like dull fog. Outflanked long before they ever understood their predicament, a tumbled retreat was the only hope of survival. Joseph saw Ike lay lifeless among the slain, forced to leave him there.

Thus emboldened the attackers pursued in frenzied blood rage. One of them would have cut Manasseh down with a high caliber deer round to the back, if it hadn't been for Joseph, who, a few feet ahead, returned fire and knocked the gunman down with a well placed shot to the shoulder first. They dove behind their truck when Manasseh realized how close the call had been.

"You're a deadeye with that repeater," he remarked breathlessly.

"I have my moments," Joseph panted.

A brief look acknowledged the magnitude of the act. They managed to climb inside and spark the engine.

The dull thud of bullets hit the sheet metal and shattered the rear window with a crash while they made their escape at breakneck speed, hard pressed to steer clear of hefty trees rooted immovably beneath the rough terrain all about.

That night Manasseh addressed Joseph before the devastated men, "You saved Ike's life, which he, in turn, valorously laid down for his friends this fateful day. I owe you the selfsame gratitude."

The brothers in arms assented.

"This kind of spirit shall see us through. Let each of us stamp out any lesser notion within themselves, just as the Judas who broke faith and betrayed us shall be, I vow it, searched and stamped out also."

Over the course of the following weeks Joseph and Miriam often found opportunities to spend time in conversation.

On one such occasion, she went to fill canisters at the spring well which supplied the base when she saw him headed the same way. Their eyes met and lit up.

After an extended stroll to a secluded clearance, where fresh dew glistened on the soft grass, Joseph laid his jacket down for them to sit on. They took in the silent serenity for some time when he asked what it was that had brought her to a place like this.

She told him how she'd been overheard in public, speaking with a friend about life and soul as present in a child from the point of conception, when a woman approached and confronted her in frantic outrage about her position, causing a scene in the street. As soon as her parents heard what had happened, they sent her away, concerned the crazed belligerent would likely report Miriam for intolerance, which could have her classified as infectious. At first she refused to leave, aware her family may be punished in her place. They however insisted, reassuring her with the promise to join up when the time was right.

Joseph listened with admiration. “I almost didn’t dare believe I’d ever meet someone like you, that I’d meet... *you*.”

She sighed and rested her head on his shoulder.

“Will your family come here?”

Miriam reached inside her coat and pulled out a folded piece of paper. "There was an artist who did landscapes of this area. My father always liked one particular work by him of a hidden valley. So much so that he decided to look into it and try to actually find the place."

She opened it up and revealed a wooded vale, bathed in gold light that broke forth from a vast sky, held up by mightful mountain peaks, like an ancient altar raised to their very Creator. From them flowed several streams into a basin below, covered in the faint glow of a mist that graced the crystalline glacier water, while a majestic buck slaked its thirst in the foreground.

"Did he?" Joseph inquired, immersed in the mystical allure the painter had captured.

"Sure did… we went almost every summer when I was little. The camper he set up should still be there. Unless it was all a dream."

He thought for a moment. "We'd never find it without a map."

Miriam turned the painting over. There was a line of digits scribbled on the back.

"Latitude and longitude…" Joseph realized.

An eremite of considerable years, cloistered someplace within those mountains longer than anyone remembered, showed up at camp on a night of heavy downpour. A black hat pulled low over his furrowed temple concealed a sunken visage. Thin veins of cold rainwater streamed down its brim onto the wolfskin that served as his overcoat.

"Elisha," Manasseh greeted him with a slight start when the unforeseen visitor drew near to the group of men gathered beneath the porch of the house. None of the dogs had announced his approach.

When he looked up, the haggard windows to his soul mirrored some cause, while he invariably struck those who beheld him as disheveled, presumably devoid of much solace or comfort.

"The very same," he replied. "I've come to collect what I'm owed."

"Ain't got it yet, but I'll make it up to you."

"Just what I'm owed. No more, no less."

Ceaseless torrent rushed through the trees against the wood of the old cabin.

"Just what you're owed then."

"I see your followers hold loyal." Elisha passed his glance over the others, including Joseph, on whom it appeared to rest for a split second longer.

"No followers here," Manasseh returned.

"This is the dawning of the third day, ordained since before darkness lay upon the face of the deep. Best make for the narrow quick, lest the price of those who tread your trail gets fixed upon your *own* head instead."

"There's plenty a price on my head as it is, oldtimer."

Some of the others snickered.

This seemed to offend, even stir the man. Any trace of the informal was now gone from his tone. "The leviathan you claim to hunt has swallowed you, but far from being spewed back into the light, you cling to its very bowels from within."

He disappeared back into the shadows to the contemptuous sneers of the rebels.

By morning the weather had cleared. Joseph ventured to a nearby creek, a spot he'd discovered not long after his arrival. Hidden by the brush and watched over only by those woodland creatures which dwelt there, it offered serene solitude.

When he stepped onto the glade, however, he discovered Elisha, fishing with a makeshift rod. Joseph turned to leave.

"Why so shy?"

The voice stopped him in his tracks. "Wouldn't want to disturb your peace, sir."

The old man looked over his shoulder and mustered him briefly, then continued to observe his line dangle in the brook. "Just out of curiosity, why make believe you belong with that curious congress of the baleful and marblehearted over yonder?"

"Not sure I catch your meaning."

"Stay for a minute and you might."

Joseph sighed to himself and submitted to the exchange. "Well, far as I can tell, we'd better stand and fight rather than just bow down and fade away as nothing."

"I'd agree with that." Elisha paused. "It's *where* you stand that will make all the difference when lightning strikes."

"That man you were so eager to condemn last night puts his life on the line for his principles."

"Willin' to put *yours* on the line for it, too, ain't he?"

Joseph began to grow impatient with how the greybeard dictated the exchange. "I don't know what your grievance is, but courage in righteousness ought to be valued."

"The plain of righteousness in those who profess not the King in truth remains unmarked by footfall like the sea of tranquility itself. Not manmade rebellion heals injury, breaks shackles or dries tears. A reborn heart does. There, the King provides relief."

"I appreciate a good riddle as much as the next man, but I'll be on my way now if you don't mind." Joseph walked off.

Elisha's words trailed after him, "Great

deception leads the many astray as hearts fail for fear of what's coming on the earth. Unlike them, you ought to look up for your salvation, not your destruction. Understand, with the Lord a day is like a thousand years and a thousand years are like a day. This *is* the dawning of the third day."

Baptized with leaves, the mountains lay covered in cold light, a vast sea of yellow, bronze and scarlet beneath the harvest heavens. There was a reverent forbearance in the autumn wind.

The carnage of the ambush they had fallen into still reverberated in Joseph's bones. He'd thought back on the things Herman used to tell him about the dread of war. Callously naive notions he had voiced to his grandfather with adolescent audaciousness pained him now. He would have given much to talk with the man. To listen. One of the wounded, a boy of only about fifteen, had been hit in the arm. The hollow point slug he took had burst apart and caused countless pieces of cartilage shrapnel to tear the surrounding tissue to shreds. It had to be taken off. Without access to proper treatment, he succumbed in agony and gave up the ghost a few days later. Joseph couldn't help but wonder if the man he shot in the shoulder had faced a similar fate. If he once suffered from a romantic estimation of bravery in combat, it was utterly remedied now.

Manasseh found him in this restless state, secluded in his room, when he announced the traitor had become known. He explained that a former comrade had set the trap and staged the vicious attack. “Castor and I used to run together. Before he formed his own crew on the other side of the range.” There was a kind of injured bitterness in his expression. “He was a good kid. You reminded me of him when you first got here.”

“Not sure I’m flattered.”

“He started out well. Somewhere along the line though… let’s say things took a different turn.”

“That’s a mild way to put it, considering he almost killed us all.”

"I guess that would be putting it mildly," Manasseh concurred. "Soon."

Miriam stood in the kitchen to wash the dirt from a handful of freshly picked potatoes. When she looked into the mirror above the sink, she suddenly saw Draven appear in the doorway. He stepped inside and confirmed the ominous sense that someone or something had shadowed her. His unfortunate appearance was none alleviated by the slight grin he flashed.

“You shouldn’t creep up like that, you scared me.” She watched the clear water turn brown and disappear into the gurgling drain in a swirl as she rubbed the spuds clean with her fingertips.

“What, little old me?” Draven leaned against the table behind her. “I’m the last thing you should be afraid of around here.”

Miriam felt his eyes on her. The hair on her neck stood up.

When she didn’t respond, he cleared his throat. “You know a girl like you simply shouldn’t be on her own in a place like this. Anyplace for that matter, but especially this one.”

Her heartbeat increased with discomfort at the conversation, thrust on her without desire or a way out. She swallowed her displeasure and forced herself to answer, “What makes you think I’m alone? I’ve got plenty of people to keep company with here.”

Draven snickered. “I’ve seen you with that Joseph joker... and I wanna caution you about it.” He waited to see what she’d say. When Miriam kept quiet again, he went on, “First of all, we don’t even really know who he is, if he’s trustworthy at all. Secondly, the guy is green. I mean a real cadette. What you need is an actual man to look out for you.”

“That hardly seems fair,” she said and wiped her forehead in a rushed motion. “He’s clearly as committed as anyone here.”

“I guess you either can’t or don’t want to

hear what I'm saying to you."

Miriam now shut the faucet and turned to face him. "What I'm saying is that I'm not interested." Backed against the sink, she did her best to appear assertive.

Draven stared at her as though her meaning went straight through him. There was a calm menace in his voice. "Sometimes we don't know what we're looking for until it's right in front of us." He stepped closer.

"Stop this, I'm uncomfortable."

"Of course you are," he pressed on. "That's because we haven't gotten comfortable yet. We can change all that." He pulled her close to inhale the scent of her hair.

“Stop!” She used all her strength to push him off.

“You wanna go that way? Be that clown's little hussy?” he yelled. “Well if you act the part you better get ready to play it out!”

Joseph heard them from upstairs and rushed down.

There was a mixture of terror and relief painted painfully on Miriam’s tender face when she saw him.

“Look who it is…” Draven remarked.

“Get away from her.”

“Or what, you gonna pull on me?”

“This is your only warning.”

Draven searched his rival's eyes for resolve. "Alright cowboy, don't hurt nobody… no need for commotion." He looked at Miriam with smug derision for a few seconds before he finally left, brushing up against Joseph as he passed. "I'll be seeing you two around."

Joseph walked her back to the trailer she stayed in. He waited for the scare to subside as they sat on the doorstep. A current of electrified longing might have forced him to gather her closely into his arms, even to never let go.

He laid his hand gently on Miriam's forearm. "You know where to find me if there's anything..." With that, he went to get up.

She grasped him before he was able.

Her deep gaze sank into his eyes as Joseph moved to kiss her. Like a poem written in snow, her mouth, cool from the evening air, melted slow against his lips. His heart ran over as she poured herself out into it.

When the raiding party had readied, darkness lay much enclosed about them. There were no stars visible that devil's hour except bicephalous Gemini, perpetual twin sentries, their candescent gaze record to all deeds man ever conspired to commit upon the earth.

"There's nothing lower than a man who would cut his brother's neck." Manasseh looked at the rebels, each ready to do his command. "Tonight, the turncoats will learn what it means to cross the unchained."

They came upon Castor's camp in an onslaught, determined to return the favor in full.

Many bloodied their hands with murder that night as they laid waste to the enemy's position. It was Joseph who shot him down and foiled his attempt at escape. He had steadied the rifle and lined up the sights, then slowly squeezed the trigger as he exhaled. Just as he'd been taught to do as a boy. The report of the shot magnified against the rockface when his target hit the ground.

He stood by as Manasseh towered over the wounded man, his massive chrome wheelgun cocked and leveled at his face. "I'd be well within my right to end you, here and now."

"What is this?" Castor asked with defiant contempt in his voice, his countenance painfully distorted from the burning lead borne through his thigh.

"Your inevitable downfall boy. You ought to know."

Back at the house he was bound in chains and locked inside a rusted cage in the basement.

The men sat around logs piled into a crackling fire and listened to Manasseh speak.

“We have reached the most horrid of prospects, that of universal technocracy, dominion by the maimed over the mutilated. Generations of unopposed lunatics and fools, suffered by the blind and careless to hurl the promises of our forefathers into despair. The flame of freedom is extinguished. Its rekindling requires profound sacrifice, hence the majority of those who prefer bondage. History however is only ever made, engraved upon fate, by the free.” A burst of sparks gushed agleam toward the night sky. “Let it be understood, our God given rights are no man’s to grant or deny, subject to no condition, nor a price to be bartered for a coward's peace in the face of tyranny.” He raised a bottle. “We honor the sacrifice of our brothers.”

Plenteous potent libation took effect as the revelry advanced and dispositions grew increasingly untethered. Draven sat in the corner. Drunk. Brooding. He watched closely when Miriam went to talk with Joseph by the fire. There was radiance in her eyes. Her smile. It fomented him. Covetousness became amplified while base thoughts toppled one another in his clouded skull, in a bid for supremacy over the man who harbored them.

Manasseh and Joseph reclined against the base of a white pine some ways off from the cabin and shared one last flask of brown liquor. The daystar, mighty luminary, gradually bathed the horizon with regal reach, dying the soft sky crimson as life commenced to stir anew in the brush around them.

"What's the endgame?" Joseph's voice stirred the silence. "Live free or die?"

"Better to die on your feet than live on your knees." Manasseh took a swig and gazed out into the open expanse. He handed over the whiskey. "Moser and the others are gonna like it out here. We'll get 'em before long."

Death loomed large over Castor as he felt little cause for hope, kept ignorant as to why he was still alive. His wound had been crudely treated but soon festered, causing impossible misery.

When Joseph overheard someone speak of the captive's critical condition, he felt the urge to see for himself.

“Come to shoot me in the back again?” Castor asked when he looked up and made the visitor out through the bars.

Joseph's stomach turned when the faint light revealed the prisoner's plight, which could only be construed as grimly inhumane. “I might.”

“Who made you the hanging judge...”

“You did, when you bushwhacked my friends like a cold blooded coward.”

“You swallowed that hook line and sinker, didn't you?” A resentful chuckle was cut short in Castor's throat when the pain shot up from his infected leg.

“I was there,” Joseph stated.

“That makes one of us. Wouldn’t take much of a dig to find none of what happened to you and yours that day had anything to do with me, or my men. Your dear leader wanted those guns, happy to walk over dead bodies for ‘em. It didn’t go his way. This is nothing but phony pretext to get even with me for leaving him.”

Joseph sat down on an empty wood crate. He felt the chill of the musty brick walls in that dungeon creep up his skin. A nimble rat rushed out from its crevice and disappeared from sight again. “You lie.”

Castor looked at him with disdain. “Fine pawn.”

“You don’t know me.”

"I know those who bury truth will swallow sand."

Joseph kept silent.

"Men are dead. I'm dying in this dump. Why? Because the likes of you won't open your eyes?"

"He told me about you," Joseph revealed. "You fought for the same thing."

"What would that be?"

"Freedom..."

Castor's gaze dropped. He spoke slowly, quietly, in recitation as if to himself, "Freedom has gone from the world, only masters and servants remain. Falsehood and perfidy reign over spiritless mankind."

For days the Sierra lay covered beneath tempestuous storms. Joseph hadn't been himself. It was as though some unknown menace had besieged his mind and threatened to uproot the very foundation he stood on. The confines of his room suffocated him when the sky broke open and flooded the valleys. He stepped outside to walk in spite of it.

Swift dusk concealed the prodigious peaks. Continuous rainfall rushed in his ears, unable to drown out thoughts that came to haunt him like unruly ravens, casting doubtful shadows beneath charcoal wings.

After some time, the soft lights of the camp vanished behind the black silhouette of the woods. Countless trees stood silent witness to an all too familiar nothingness that began to close in.

Miriam. The image of her redirected him.

His coat and boots were drenched by the time he got to her trailer and knocked softly against the window. She drew back the curtain from within. Surprised to see Joseph in the rain, she motioned for him to come around to the entrance and unlocked the door.

A woodstove's warmth and sweetly resinous, balsamic fragrance stood in stark contrast to the cold, wet dark without. The girl Miriam shared the place with greeted him, then excused herself to the other room to give them space.

"You've gotta get those rags off." She helped him out of his jacket and shoes and placed them near the fire, then laid a blanket over his shoulders.

"What were you doing out there?"

Joseph told her about the events of the past days, about what had happened in retaliation for the ambush, about the conversation with Castor and how it was all he could think about since. "There was something right about him." He stared into the flames.

Miriam poured some coffee. "Don't you owe it to yourself, let alone the man in that cage, to heed your intuition on this?"

He took the pleasantly warm tin cup between his hands. "Intuition won't count for much if I go against Manasseh."

"How could you do otherwise if you know the thing to be wrong," she stated more than asked.

“I don’t think you understand how things work in this place.”

“Not much of it…” She paused. “And I’m grateful to be able to be here, but I understand that you tell a tree by its fruit and I know someone hard of heart when I see them.”

“Hard of heart?”

“A person may be convinced they’re doing what’s right, when in truth they might be seduced and blinded by pride. They elevate and exalt themselves over others, instead of falling on God’s grace. There’s impropriety in a man like that.”

Joseph shifted in his seat. “Considering what’s going on in the world, I don’t think it’s right to talk like that about the few people left who stand up for our dignity.”

He set the coffee down.

"Like the dignity of the man you captured?" Miriam asked. "Dignity comes from Jesus Christ, but I haven't heard anyone in this camp concerned with that. If you see someone purposely lead people contrary to His will, it begs the question of whether they haven't in fact made an idol of themselves. I honestly wouldn't know how you and I could have a future if you went along with it."

"Maybe we were too quick to assume that we *do* have a future together in the first place." Immediately after anger forced those words out of his mouth, they ached down to his very core.

"Maybe we were." Her eyes welled up as he stepped into his boots, grabbed his coat and left.

Manasseh and a few others sat and laughed about something when Joseph walked in. As if it were the last recourse before he became entombed in a loss of conviction, he addressed him directly, "There's something we need to discuss."

The men went quiet.

"Take a seat. You should be here anyway."

"This can't wait." Deadlock tension filled the room as his openly defiant insistence echoed across several seconds of silence.

Manasseh perceived Joseph wasn't going to let up. He yielded if only to avoid embarrassment. "Well, urgent is urgent, I guess. Excuse us, boys."

Once the others had left the room, Joseph sat down. “I believe the man beneath us, dying in a cage as we speak, might not be who you think he is. If that’s true, I can’t have his blood on my hands.”

Manasseh’s demeanor morphed from yet patient requiescence to a hardened restraint, as in reaction to sudden provocation. “It’s a tad late for that, wouldn’t you say?”

Joseph’s lack of response pressed his point.

“I appreciate the doubtlessly noble desire for unstained hands. We have men dead and gone however. As far as *their* blood is concerned, that traitor down in that basement is drenched in it. The whirlwind is in the thorn tree for him. He knew the cost.”

“We’ve got to carefully consider the consequences of what we decide to do here,” Joseph urged earnestly.

“What *we* decide…” Manasseh scratched his chin. “You’ll know something about consequences when every step you take makes or breaks everything around you, all of what those who put their trust in you sacrificed for. When you chose to join yourself to this cause you did more than cast your lot in with a handful of weekend rebels for kicks. You became part of a brotherhood unto death.” He fixated Joseph with his eyes. “We stand with our brothers, to the end, come what may.”

“Have I not proved my dedication?”

“Indeed. More than most. You read the signs of the times and possess the heart to act on them. What you *don’t* yet have is the humility that comes with being forced to accept, though you can't always make the right choice, you've got to make the best one available. So far, the men here look to me to guide them out of the bondage and misery they've been subjected to. You may like the way I do that or you may not, but you know I *will* do it, to my very last breath." He allowed his words to resonate. "War is a solemn and religious matter… it comes to make its children desolate, lawless, hateful. You must enshrine the thing you're in it for."

Autumn was brief, its forlorn beauty obliterated as frost covered the range with deathful dominion. Glacier lakes reflected light like ghostly mirrors, all life therein enclosed beneath a vast seal, flanked by white mountaintops which appeared as mere hills at that altitude, if one hadn't known the abysmal depth reaching down their colossal backs. The only color left were the conifers, barely visible beneath thick snowfall. Birds departed south and left the endless wild blue to the few stubborn crows that chose to stay.

Joseph's breath rose in steam before his eyes. He looked out across the reservoir. The thought of Castor wasting away wouldn't let him rest. Walking, even for hours on end, offered none of its usual relief.

It was early morning when his exhausted mind finally gave way to brief sleep, during which a dream, unlike any he'd ever known, impressed itself upon him. Moved to tears by images still present the moment he awoke, Joseph felt the urge to share it with Miriam. The pain of how they'd parted burned like a red hot iron against his heart when he got himself up to look for her.

She had busied herself with menial tasks. Nevertheless, a forthright nature only allowed for so much sorrow to remain concealed. Alleviation shone kindled in the gleam of her eyes when she saw him walk up. The relief he felt when he found her equally eager to ameliorate was like the recovery of the lost key to some hidden gate, behind which the promise of life lay locked away in a secret garden.

"I had a dream..." He sat down on her couch. "A large cloud, quite close, shone with a sublime glow from its center, like God Himself stood on the other side, slowly advancing through towards me as it grew brighter and brighter. I was suddenly raised from the ground. A tremendous burden shed from me with every inch I ascended. The relief, the joy was indescribable…" Joseph's gaze became distant.

"It sounds like the Lord returning for His people. He's calling you."

"Calling me to what? What am I supposed to do?"

"Ask… seek… knock… He *will* answer."

Desperate to believe, Joseph wanted it to be true when Manasseh summoned and informed the men that a meeting with Sothis, the mayor of Repentance, was a strategic necessity, indispensable for the effective continuation of their efforts.

"Some of you will have a hard time with the thought of negotiations. I know it." He pulled out the heavy revolver with its mother of pearl handle, the cylinder blackened from burnt powder, and raised it above his head. "This!" he exclaimed. "This is what got us here." He cocked the hammer and fired a booming shot into the ice blue sky, the report of which scattered the crows from their barren trees.

The men cheered as he slid the gun back into his belt.

"There is a time for war. There is also a

time for words. Who would the burden come to rest on if we failed to seize the moment granted us, here and now, to advance our sacred duty into the future, by any and all means? Let no one say, those men sought to achieve with brute force what only cunning forbearance could accomplish, and failed us."

Radiant sunshine stood in stark contrast to the crisp cold air all day, blanketing the range magenta, reflected by the snow in a resplendent play of light. To the astonishment of the men, the mayor arrived alone except for his driver, who opened the rear passenger door.

They stood on the porch and watched their sworn adversary climb out of the car. He strolled toward the house with a smile that seemed to disarm and threaten simultaneously with unnatural equanimity.

“Them aware of our position like this... it’s all kinds of wrong,” the man next to Joseph mumbled in a low voice while he kept his eyes fixed ahead.

Sothis tipped an imaginary hat. “The Range o’Light Rebels in the flesh… whoever thought I’d see the day.” He passed them and followed Manasseh inside.

They took their seats across from one another at the roundtable while the others stood or sat fanned out across the room.

“Nice place you’ve got here,” the mayor remarked and looked around. “Real steal I bet.”

“We like to consider it more of a donation to the cause,” Manasseh returned.

“Tax deductible! Not my favorite. But then I’m just a humble public servant. In contrast, you fellers have made quite a reputation for yourselves lately. Images in people’s heads, stories floating around… real folklore like. There’s no denying the odd conspiracy minded basement dweller is kept up at night with musings of what it’d be like to throw caution to the wind and ride with Manasseh’s notorious outlaws. But the simple fact remains, to the acquiescent citizenry, you all are a menace, the reason their much coveted supplies can’t be counted on for punctual delivery. In short, a nuisance. Now I’ll be a son of a gun if that hasn't served to rally the good folk of this proud land behind yours truly, committed as I am to the protection of their vital interests, especially during voting season." He gave an election poster grin. "I'm not too blind to see this sort of publicity works both ways. So we may speak of a kind of symbiotic reciprocity. Some might even reckon it the makings of a mutually beneficial enterprise."

"No telling what some might do."

"Indeed. Here's what you *can* tell though. There's a storm coming. A federal crackdown. The kind which won't leave too many of the likes of you on their feet once it sweeps through these picturesque peaks and valleys you call home. Granted that's a grim picture, fighting words to your noble warrior hearts no doubt." He leaned forward. "But I haven't come to pick fights. On the contrary, I've always said, sensible men ought to explore and exhaust all avenues of diplomacy before they cross the line of no return."

The casual air with which Sothis issued his threat in that lion's den was an open affront to the men, causing perceptible unease.

"Now look here, I'm aware you and a handful of other renegade outfits have been at each other's throats. I'm also aware you're running dangerously low on ammo." An ever so slight hint of pleasure formed in the sides of his mouth as he observed the subtle, involuntary reaction to his possession of sensitive information. "I know that because we've bought it all up. All of it. From here to hades and back."

"I've got at least one bullet left," one of them finally muttered.

Manasseh cautioned the man to hold his peace with a brief gesture.

"Nice touch," the mayor replied. He assumed a conciliatory tone. "And that may be all you need indeed. But why force the battle when you can shape the war? I will grant you boys amnesty from the federal hit squads, which, believe you me, they're a comin', as sure as a wild goose never laid a tame egg. On top of that I will share with you, out of the embarrassment of riches that is our armory. You'll continue to hold your own, with significant advantage over your rivals. Now correct me if I'm wrong, but I don't see you make it through the winter any other way. All I ask in return is that you leave off from the transports coming to my town until further notice. What you do with other routes is none of my business. I may also call on your active support against the less reasonable parties in these parts from time to time. Speaking of which, I'll require the prisoner you've got here."

Stunned, Joseph spoke up, "How do you know about him?"

"Chalk it up to mayor's intuition. He's alive, I hope?"

Manasseh nodded.

"Well then! Let me draw the line before I pontificate myself all the way to perdition. I'll give you gentlemen some time to mull it over." With that, he got up and exited the house.

"We're in no position to pass up munitions," Draven asserted.

"He's bluffing, the feds are spread far too thin to make it up here," another remarked.

They awaited their leader's verdict when Manasseh addressed Draven with a simple "get it done."

Soon after, Joseph watched from his room's window as they pushed the stumbling Castor to the mayor's car. They opened the trunk, shoved the prisoner inside and slammed it shut.

I've got to do something, Joseph thought.

He hurried down the stairs, out of the back of the building and uncovered a snowmobile from under a tarp. The key was in the ignition. He revved it up, then cut through a narrow path in the woods until he reached an elevated point where the road lay visible beneath him. If they had taken the way he counted on, he'd be able to follow them from there under cover of the trees.

The engine bubbled as the exhaust rose into the cold air. He fixed his eyes on the point where the lane disappeared behind a sharp turn. "Come on…" he implored, his grip tight on the quivering handles.

About to second guess his choice and turn around to go another way, he heard the faint drone of a vehicle crunch the snow beneath its tires. He tensed up until they finally pulled around the corner.

Careful to keep enough distance, he stayed on them. They took serpentines which, to Joseph's surprise, led higher and further up into the range as opposed to back down toward the highway. The snowmobile suddenly failed to accelerate as he twisted the throttle in vain. His heart dropped when the machine slowed until it came to a full stop and forced him to watch the car trail off and disappear. The gas gauge had fallen below empty some time ago. He got up, cursed and kicked the mirror off the frame.

The sun was going to set soon. In his rush he had taken nothing with him. No knife or gun, not even a coat. If he got lost and failed to make it back, he would most certainly freeze to death.

Looking back and forth between the two directions, he decided to press on afoot.

The fresh snow would allow him to make out their trace, at least until day retreated behind the mountains.

Joseph followed the tracks to where they had left the road and shifted onto a path through private land. Sepulchral darkness swiftly engulfed all things as Sirius burned enthroned in a frozen sky, casting his fevered omen over the soundless nightscape.

He began to wonder if he'd made a fatal blunder in his persistence when he perceived a small light some ways in the distance. Relief was marred with apprehension of what lay ahead.

Doing his best to ignore the increasing numbness of his hands and feet, Joseph finally made out an elaborate wood and stone country residence. He approached carefully and scaled the adjacent hillside to gain view of its yard, which lay enclosed and sheltered from sight by a grove of tall winter pines.

What he beheld next appeared more rooted in delirium than actuality. Gathered in front of a massive stone beast, bull faced humanoid at least twenty five feet tall, there stood about a dozen figures, robed in what looked like ceremonial attire, the pale moonshine cold silver against their silhouette.

One of them ascended a scaffold in front of the statue and began to speak. "We gather tonight, disciples of old faith, adherents to that beacon of unconquered will of ages past, shining forth since before the formation of our plane, the bright morning star. That most brilliant light of lights still illumines the oppressive bleakness of predetermined existence, binding us one to another in this, our eternal bond."

"In bond eternal," the others answered in unison.

"Even a plan that stretches across millennia will, followed diligently, one day reach its stage of fulfillment. Behold the splendid fruit borne through monolithic devotion of the faithful. Those who know, see. We the privileged, witnesses to the quickening of Apollyon's ascent, salute you."

The speaker got down on his knees facing the graven image, then bowed to the ground and repeated the motion five times before he stood back up to continue.

"What distinguishes us is the dismantlement of the empyrean despot's framework, the inversion of the pillars, voluntarily carried out by the fools who would have found shelter therein to withstand our purpose. The notion of unity between the head and the body of a house has been made into a stifled symbol, a relic of the past, odorous profanity to be discarded, rubbed out without pity, without vestige. Point to a place in public perception where depiction of masculine virility and feminine nurture in their original form are still accepted, let alone embraced or celebrated. You cannot, because they are outcast to the reprehensible recess of illegitimate bygones. Instead, one seeks to replace itself with the other, each utterly undone in the process. Seed is cut off at the root by those who would bear it, to the laudation of the only ones that could have protected it. Of their own free will, they elect death over life. To the uninitiated observer our progress in recent time appears sudden, even radical, when the true disarmament of them that would oppose us has progressed slowly, corrosively at first, as a small ax fells a mighty oak, until down is up and up is down, where all find themselves fated to fall to our great predation. Spiritual crisis occurs in your opponent once you succeed in their fundamental separation from natural identity, indeed from the very source thereof. Such a crisis reaches so deep, the ensuing disorientation so far, that the subject of your efforts will join in the labor of their own desolation, without cease and unto completion. Behold, man now stands alone, isolated, not posed to uplift but to debase, not to build but to destroy, not to hallow, but to defile. And where the distant echo of a soul yet calls for freedom, we will be there to answer, fear not, for you *shall* be free, to do as we command."

The group withdrew into the house when a handful of servants shuffled out. They carried materials with which they set about the construction of some kind of pyre. Once they were done, they disappeared, only to reemerge shortly afterward with Castor, whom they pulled to the stone abomination and left there, motionless in the snow.

A strange, dull sound resonated from behind the walls of the building, reminiscent of ancient chants, only no redemptive quality could be felt to emanate from the sinister sequence of notes, the intervals of which instead conveyed a brooding, unholy menace.

When the coast was clear Joseph climbed down the hillside, over a wall and onto the premises. He stayed in the shadows until he reached Castor, who looked up in dazed confusion when Joseph took the gag from his mouth.

“You?”

“Whatever this is,” Joseph answered, “we’re getting out of it.” He struggled with the ropes around Castor’s wrists and ankles until they came undone. “Let’s go!”

“I can’t walk on this leg… it’s all rotten...” There was an almost cold, hopeless apathy in his voice now. The fervor had gone from his eyes.

“We’ve just gotta get over that hill.” Joseph laid Castor’s arm across his shoulder and lifted him.

The man groaned with anguish. His head fell back as he slipped to the verge of consciousness.

“Stay with me.”

They began to make their way toward the wall when something moved behind them. Joseph turned to find a man with a gun leveled at him.

The sentry called in the intrusion over the radio. They were forced to kneel and zip tied when Mayor Sothis walked out toward them. “How kind of you to visit,” he addressed Joseph. “Unfortunately, it’s more of an invite only type shindig.”

The unhallowed congregation reassembled. Joseph looked on as Castor was bound to the stake.

The odious orator's words cut into the backdrop of the night, reverberating his heinous homily. "Will opposed to our will is forbidden. Scorched in the power." His outstretched arm pointed at Castor. "Just so, we commit to the flame this symbol of defiant spirit."

A ghoulish exhibition commenced as the pyre was lit, causing the fuel drenched materials piled beneath him to ignite in a violent burst. The man now found himself engulfed in the reality of his earthly end, made immolated oblation to some profane idol at the hands of his enemies. The ensuing sight, sound and stench of the unnatural act perpetrated there would no doubt curse the soil of that sacrilegious place until the end of time.

When it was finally finished, a grotesquely desecrated, charred figure was all that remained where the image bearer of a divine Maker had been. Joseph's mind was forced into dullness at the murderous derangement he'd witnessed. He expected to die next.

"What about that one?" a servant asked Sothis and gestured toward Joseph.

"Take him back where he came from."

"You're letting him go, sir? After what he's seen?"

The mayor looked at the serf with cold repulsion in his eyes, as though by questioning a direct order he had all but forfeited his own life. At that, the man quickly grabbed Joseph and dragged him away.

"Is it wise?" one of the robed figures reiterated the concern.

The light of the slowly dying flames danced on Sothis' face. "It'll give that mountain mongrel a chance to prove his dependability."

It had been three days and nights in the same rusty cage he had stood on the other side of not long ago. Joseph was plagued with relentless night terror.

Utterly exhausted, a recurring incubus haunted him as soon as he would drift off to sleep. It was always the same. Castor in front of his gun sights just before he pulls the trigger, looking straight at him. Sudden cognizance of the deadly error he's about to commit overcomes Joseph with clarity that pierces his conscience, but his hand fails to obey. It mechanically squeezes the trigger. The blast rings out. Dropping the rifle in the dirt, he runs over to help, but Castor's body goes up in a ferocious blaze. Joseph is forced to back off from the searing heat and look on. At this point he would be ripped from his troubled daze in cold sweat, his heaving chest unable to contain his breath.

Over and over, he would wake to none of the relief other nightmares offered in the gradual assurance of their utter divorce from reality. Instead his mind lay bare, torn by things that should never have come to pass.

There was no daylight in that basement. No small window or crack through which it might have entered. Even just the glimmer of a ray would have given him comfort. He craved the sight of the mountains and the satisfaction of crisp air in his lungs like he never knew possible. The thought of Miriam alone in this place, without him there to watch over her, convulsed his spirit with agony when he heard the wooden floorboards creak at someone's approach. One part of him shrunk back whilst the other insisted on dignified collectedness in the face of whatever emerged from the shadows.

It was her. Joseph rushed forward and gripped the bars. An avalanche of emotion overcame them as she hurried down and grasped his hands. Their kiss became saline with her tears.

“How did you get in?” Joseph asked.

“That monster Draven has been guarding the basement since they brought you here. I couldn’t come earlier…” Pain charged with indignant rage trembled in her voice. “He’s gone today. The other one let me in… thank God!” She took something from her pocket. It was Joseph's Bible. “Look…” she said, “I found this in your room.” Tears began to roll down her face again.

His words failing, he reached behind her head and pulled her close to kiss her once more.

"What happened?" she asked with whispered desperation.

"Something terrible…" Joseph fought to keep his composure.

"*What is it?"* her eyes seemed to inquire.

He didn't answer.

Miriam ran her hand over his hair. "What should I do?"

At that moment the door swung open. Draven burst in. "Get out of here!" he barked and bolted toward them. There was a cattle prod in his hand, with which he threatened to strike Miriam when she wouldn't budge from the cage.

"I'll kill you!" Joseph reached his arm through the bars to grab hold of him.

Draven in turn rammed the prod into his chest and gave him a blast of electric current which threw Joseph backward onto the concrete floor.

"No!" Miriam screamed and attempted to wrest the torture device from him.

He struck and caused her to bend down in pain.

"You'll die for this," Joseph said quietly.

Draven sneered. "Well then I better make the most of it." He dragged her away and up the stairs.

Struggling to resist, she turned her head. "I'll come back! I'll come back for you!"

The door slammed shut behind them.

Joseph no longer took note of the dark in his eyes, nor the cold in his bones, when Manasseh came down to him on the sixth day. He pulled up a chair next to the cage, assessing the unfortunate state of his protege turned prisoner.

"For those of any concern to myself do I wish bleak desolation, that they might grow familiar with self contempt, the pain of doubt, the torment of the conquered. I've got no pity for them, because I wish them the one thing that proves if anyone is worth the dirt they walk on, to endure…" He paused. "I read those words in a book once. But this… this was never meant to happen."

Joseph remained mute.

"I suppose you find me weighed and wanting." Manasseh produced a flask from the inside pocket of his big fur coat and extended it towards the bars. When there was still no response, the man twisted off the cap and took a deep draft himself. He clenched his teeth and pulled a sharp breath through them as the liquor burned its way down his chest. “It doesn’t serve anyone to make things more complicated than they need be. Which is what you’ve gone and done. I by contrast did what I had to. For us.”

“I wonder how long the others will buy that line.”

“The others will know what’s good for them. They’ll see the place I’ve afforded us in the future that’s come to be. As for them who don’t... the wheel of history’s in motion. Some will doubtlessly find themselves poorly positioned as it waltzes by.”

Joseph finally turned his head toward the man he thought he knew so well. “What did they *really* offer you?”

“I don’t expect you to understand the nuances leadership comes to require of a man. You ain’t got the years.” He screwed the whiskey shut and put it back in its place. “If we are free, it's because we have the courage to bleed for it.”

“Like Castor.” The crestfallen disillusion in Joseph’s tone was so wounded and final, it couldn’t be evaded by either of them.

“The voice you hear, I used to hear it myself, but it’s been tongue tied. A deaf void when I needed it most. The day she went away, that’s when it quit on me. Then what? Was I supposed to quit, too?”

Stillness filled the damp, dark room.

“The stars are aligned for us to seize. You had the grit to stand up to me. I respect that. Now have the sense to stand down.”

“Those who bury the truth will swallow the sand,” Joseph answered.

Manasseh looked at him for a prolonged moment. “So be it.” He got up.

When he had reached the top of the stairs, he turned back one last time. “No great height without terrible depth.” With that, he stepped out and disappeared.

His limbs sore from confinement, Joseph was unaware if it was day or night until they marched him out beneath a pearl blue sky that burned his eyes all the way to the pit. There it lay gaping the earth, callously impartial, unchanged from the time he'd seen it when he first arrived.

"Sorry about this," he heard the voice behind him mutter.

The pain he felt when the butt of a rifle cracked into his spine and caused him to stumble forward vanished the very next moment, when his body crashed face down onto the bottom of that frozen abyss, a little less than twenty feet below, where he blacked out.

The sun was long gone. In its stead a sickle moon lay slanted over the summits of the Sierra, bathing them sapphirine in a misted hue. Joseph pulled the crisp air into his lungs and held his breath as he rolled over slowly onto his back. He lay still like that for a while, his mind curiously clear. The phosphorescent gloom of night revealed the Seven Sisters, which appeared to surge above the blackness of the world unanchored.

Soon the muscle tissue around his bruised ribs pulsed with dull discomfort. Barely able to rise, he felt his way along the walls for any protrusion that might have served to pull himself up on. Nothing. An attempt to call for help only brought forth a painful gasp.

He sat down with careful strain. The admittance of his predicament crept forth like a foul substance set to drown any redemptive notion. Something in his pocket pushed against his leg. *The Bible...* Joseph rested his forehead against it. "Is this Your will?" He looked up at the firmament.

Drops of thawed snow plinked against the rock with incessant consistency like some crude Mephistophelian clock. The night wind moved above, endless elemental seesaw rushing back and forth unseen. When at last he opened the black leatherbound Book at random, faint starlight illumined the words on the page.

Let the wicked forsake his way, and the unrighteous man his thoughts: and let him return unto the LORD, and he will have mercy upon him, for he will abundantly pardon.

With nowhere else to retreat, nowhere to turn, something within finally broke.

Joseph hung his head and wept tears of lamentation. His hands clasped in prayer before his face so firmly his knuckles turned white, he spoke with his eyes pressed shut.

"I am guilty Lord… guilty of vile offense against You. I deserve Your punishment. I deserve hell for breaking Your law… please… don't let me come before You like this. Jesus… forgive me. Take my soul into Your hands..."

Time dissolved into an untraceable moment when, in sudden omnitude, the pit shone illumined with unworldly fire, a radiance so amplified, it forced Joseph's averted gaze.

His heart almost failed as he sensed a personal presence emanating power and benevolence of a harmonious magnitude he had not previously understood to exist. He began to perceive, through no immediate comprehension of his own, that he was in the presence of a holy messenger.

The angelic voice resounded like pearls poured out onto precious metal, veiled in the rush of a thousand waters,

"FEAR YE NOT, STAND STILL, AND SEE THE SALVATION OF THE LORD, WHICH HE WILL SHEW TO YOU TODAY. FOR THE SON OF MAN IS COME TO SEEK AND TO SAVE THAT WHICH WAS LOST."

Silence set back in.

Awash in ineffable love, Joseph lifted his eyes slowly and saw a soft amber luminescence in places on the wall of the cave, marking an unseen path upwards with points for his hands to grasp and his feet to step on. He climbed.

Once emerged, he fell to his knees and thanked his God with ardent solemnity.

Cautious to keep behind the white edge of the forest by the nascent advance of dawn, he realized they had broken camp, most likely to move to the winter base.

When he reached Miriam's trailer, it too stood abandoned, the door left thrown open. The painting she'd shown him was still there. He looked at the digits on the back and slid it into his pocket.

It was doubtful they would have left at night, so they were probably still close. Joseph gathered any useful supplies he could find and started after them.

The mighty trunk of an uprooted pine lay crashed across the road, halting the rebel's convoy in its tracks when he came upon them. A group of men, among them Manasseh and Draven, stood by in apparent conference over how to proceed. Joseph had no plan. He simply walked toward them. His calm, steady pace belied how he was left to die by those he had counted most trusted, as though none of it had occurred, or if it did, that it was of no further relevance to what would happen now. Sober resolution stood cut into his countenance. They turned, bewildered as they noticed him.

Draven raised his rifle and took aim.

Only Manasseh perceived the seraphic guardian that followed closely behind Joseph. It compelled him, irresistibly, to lay his hand on the barrel of Draven's gun and push it back down slowly, in silent anticipation.

Miriam emerged from one of the trucks and ran past them toward the one she had feared lost forever.

"No you don't." Draven grabbed her arm and yanked her back.

"Let them go." Manasseh's voice was subdued, as though the words were only afterthought to some deeper impact, some sudden, fearful reverence overpowering him.

Draven instead tightened his grip on Miriam's arm and looked at his commander with an amalgam of doubt and disgust, a shadow of murderous defiance aflash in his eyes, until Manasseh repeated himself with muted urgency, "I said let them go."

Miriam tore herself away and ran into Joseph's arms.

"Are you okay?" he asked.

"I'm fine."

They walked away.

Manasseh watched after them until they had disappeared entirely out of sight.

He noticed a piece of paper in the snow where Joseph had stood and picked it up.

It was a painted landscape with coordinates written on the back.

The Range of Light Rebels reached their destination that night beneath a barren sky, opaque with dull fog.

It wasn't long after they had settled that Draven, with a few others, approached Manasseh, who stood in front of the fireplace in his quarters. Unspoken animosity supplanted the reverence with which he was usually addressed, a foul odor of ill will discernible to some special sense common to man and animal alike.

"It was a mistake." Any further conversation was now a burdensome delay of more definitive means to Draven. It was beyond the restrictions of his nature to tolerate the humiliation he had tasted in the denial of his base, albeit profound desire.

"A mistake..." Manasseh echoed absentmindedly.

"You shouldn't have let them leave. I'll find 'em. They ain't got too far yet. I'll find 'em and make it right."

Manasseh knew Draven had perceived his act as weak, that he would go after them to kill Joseph and return Miriam, even if ordered otherwise.

"We can double back and put the dogs on 'em," one of the men chimed in.

Draven gave a short nod, as if to force the matter to a close already.

Manasseh spoke into the glowing heat, “A man’s need for truth, neglected over time, has a way of growing into a thick hedge of thorn around his heart, ultimately impenetrable to the moral knowledge inscribed thereon, until it, condemned to petrification, is little more than a tombstone, engraved with hateful commemorations. You and I… are cursed with such a heart.”

With that, he committed the painting Joseph had lost to the flames. Slowly engulfed, it curled up and dissolved into ashes. He walked over to the door, which he proceeded to lock. By the time he turned, the look on his face left little doubt as to his intent. He drew a knife from the back of his belt and fell on the startled men with all the ferocity of a cornered lion. One after the other dropped to the ground. Only Draven managed to pull his pistol and fire into Manasseh's abdomen before the blade was plunged into his neck. Their eyes met one last time when Manasseh took the gun from Draven's hand and shot him through the chest with dull pragmatism, like one putting his rabid dog out of its misery. Then the rebel chieftain fell among the dead.

Joseph and Miriam set up a makeshift camp. He held her reclined in his embrace after they had gathered and lit some firewood.

“Tomorrow we’ll make our way to the valley.” Reaching into his pocket, his fingers came up empty. He shot up and began to turn his bag inside out.

“What’s wrong?”

“I had it, I had the painting! I went to get it from your camper before I…” He looked around frantically.

“It’s alright.” Miriam pulled up her sleeve to reveal the numbers written on her forearm.

Joseph lept down, grabbed her and planted a firm kiss on her cheek with a loud smack. “You’re brilliant.”

She smiled. “They forced me to leave before I could find you, so I left the painting in case you looked for me there.”

Despite their combined temperature in a thermal bedroll, the piercing cold forced them to press on early while the landscape still shimmered crystalline like countless diamonds strewn across the earth.

Following map and compass, they kept a steady pace until they finally reached a glade that overlooked the vale, now covered in snow.

Miriam found her bearings and led them to the place where her father's camper had been. There it stood.

"It's here!" she exclaimed.

The key lay hidden in the same place underneath the wheel cover it had always been.

Inside they discovered that the man who had often spoken to her about the importance of prudent preparedness had not fallen short of his own words. It was dry and well insulated, equipped with a woodstove oven, blankets, essential tools, a rifle with plenty of munition, books containing crucial information, diverse canned goods to sustain at least four people over several months and a well stocked store of medical supplies. There were even seeds for food plants.

Set to sit out the remainder of the winter, they settled into their hidden home.

Rising with the sun daily was followed by the study of Holy Scripture and prayer. In the evenings they sat by the fire and talked or shared the pleasurable quiet before they concluded the day with the Our Father. A natural rhythm carried them through.

Tranquil composure was only disrupted when Joseph thought back, not of his own volition, on Castor and his gruesome end. In those moments he found himself beleaguered by implications of his instrumentality in the man's demise. He would relive the horror he'd witnessed, intently combing it over and over for anything he may have done differently, as though he might yet somehow alter the past. Pondering Castor's lot in contrast to his own fortune, he failed to understand why God had spared him so.

The only thing which would restore peace was Miriam's calm empathy in reminding him that God's forgiveness toward His contrite children, His washing away of their sins, is absolute and everlasting. How the Lord chooses to forget their trespasses and replaces them with His Son's perfect, imputed righteousness, covered in which the born again believer will stand glorified before His throne, and that the fate of the living as well as the dead, rests immovably in His incomprehensible might.

When the snow finally began to melt it made way for brimming color saturated with aureate sunlight, stirred by the tender balm of the wind, all of it earth's regenerative bestowment upon mankind. Spring.

The valley was thus revealed as the unsurpassed source of inspiration the artist had drawn from when he rendered that secludedly edenesque parcel of creation.

Time passed with careless motion in an idyll that should, by all reckoning of their human hearts, have lasted forever.

Joseph's senses lingered in the moment as he passed through a hushed meadow, laid out beneath a dazed sky, lit as though through emerald stained glass. Tall, lush grass caressed the skin of his bare feet. Wild blooms emanated their mild scent and the rush of a nearby stream called him like the faint song of some benign siren.

There she was. The glacial water glistened on the slender curves of Miriam’s figure.

Joseph laid himself down by the bank, closed his eyes and drifted away while a melody in her velvet voice carried over.

He slept like a child until the outline of a dream began to form. Dark gloom hung over the town he saw. Two figures were on the move toward him, they pushed against a strong tempest in a struggle for every step. The black at their backs drew closer, set to engulf and devour them with steadfast indifference. *Joseph…* He heard his name called, muffled by the rushing wind. *Joseph!* Then he recognized them. It was Pastor Moser, followed closely by Aaron.

When he woke, the clouds had been dyed indigo gray, quiet thunder rolling in their bowels with the promise of summer rain.

Hesitant, Joseph gave in to Miriam's repeated inquiry as to the cause of his downcast spirit some days later. He finally revealed the vision, oppressive premonition, which had hovered over him like a ghost.

"You told me you know some men on the reservation outside Repentance," she recalled. "Might they not help?"

"I've seen enough violence… and what about all this? We're happy here."

"You're right. I am happy, more than ever… but how could I live with myself, if I were the reason you refused God's call?"

"I might never return."

Miriam reflected for some time. "My sister and I used to sit in our room on those long nights when my father and the men from church met in our den. They'd pour over Scripture and look for ways to deal with matters at hand. I often listened with my ears pressed to the wall. One time they spoke about the temptation of the Lord, the satanic vision in the desert, offering contentment, the apparent fulfillment of His ministry without the cross, in exchange for abandonment of the Father's will. It *is* beautiful here, but doesn't that passage apply to us now? If the devil was able to present such a lure to the Lord Himself, there's no telling what he might try with us. Jesus showed us how to resist, by the power of His Word."

Joseph saw love in her eyes he now realized he'd only barely begun to comprehend.

Leaving the mountain they reached the boundless monotony of wasteland, anvil to the mighty sun, threatening to crush menaced mortals beneath its untempered relentlessness.

With carefully prepared rations of water and proper cover from the heat, they made it to the rancheria.

Maddox welcomed the weary wayfarers with joyous surprise.

That evening, after they had rested and caught up over a hearty meal, Joseph explained his intention to liberate Pastor Moser, supposing he was still alive, along with the others.

“There might be serious risk involved,” Maddox considered.

“I don’t ask for help lightly. I’ll understand if you can’t go.”

“If your God has sent you here then I don’t want to miss out on His plan. Besides, I’ve never been one to turn down a good bit of excitement. Give me a few days, I might just have an idea how we can pull this off.”

The desert lay Martian in its unpeopled vastitude. It had a way of purifying a man’s senses with silence, required to discern the merit of one's inward murmuration. Joseph used the time to fast and pray in preparation for what was to come.

The sky was so clear that they could see their shadows by the soft glow of the milky way the night they left.

Miriam stayed behind with old Winston and his wife as Joseph and Maddox went into Repentance.

Aaron almost didn't believe his eyes when he saw his friend in the darkness of the road, tossing pebbles at his window just like they'd done as kids.

"You came back..." he whispered as he opened the door.

They greeted each other with brotherly affection. Spud shot out past Aaron and jumped up on Joseph, whimpering with his little white tail wagging uncontrollably. He chuckled and took a knee to scratch him behind the ears. "Hey ol'boy, you holdin' up?" There was comfort in the presence of Herman's trusty companion.

"Where's the pastor?"

"They've still got him." Aaron sounded as though he himself was guilty of the man's prolonged predicament.

"They'll kill him in there. We've gotta get him out," Joseph stated.

"He'd have to leave town with his family."

"Not just them. You and the others, too. I found a place we can go. Call them and tell those that choose to come to get ready now and meet us at the westward road by the edge of town when the fireworks start."

"Fireworks?"

"Just tell them."

Pastor Moser sat in solitary confinement of the psych ward and spoke through the slit in the door with his guard, a man he'd become acquainted with since his detention. Around this time, during which there was no other personnel present in that wing of the institution, was when he usually asked Moser all types of questions, sometimes intently listening to his answers for hours on end.

“Tell me the bad news again,” the guard prompted him.

“God’s divine judgment is as the raging black sea, which must drink down into terrible depth the souls of all who elect prideful enmity over humble reconciliation with their Holy Maker. We are all transgressors of divine law, every last one, deserving of the Creator’s just punishment.”

“Now the good.”

"God is both perfectly just, so that no offense is able to go unpunished, and perfectly loving, so that, in spite of our transgression, He does not wish to see us suffer nor perish. In order to reconcile His justice with His love, He has offered Himself in His Son, Jesus Christ, so that He has received the punishment for the sin of the world in our place, paying our judicial debt with His own sacred blood. If we accept and embrace His self sacrifice by putting our faith in the Son of God, believing that He died on the cross for us and rose from the dead on the third day, we escape His righteous anger and are admitted back into His loving presence, eternal life, saved by faith alone, justified not by our works, but by His grace."

"He'll even make us His children, partakers in His glory forever…" the man reiterated a previous exchange.

"Correct."

At that moment Joseph and Aaron managed to break into the back entrance of the building. The alarm rang out as they made their way up to the floor where Moser was held. The warden saw them and pulled the gun from his waist.

"We mean you no harm." They raised their hands in the hope to avoid physical confrontation.

"Aaron, is that you?" the pastor called from behind the door of his cell.

The guard understood who they had come for and lowered his weapon. He unlocked the door and looked at Moser. "Let me go with you."

Meanwhile, Maddox set about his task. Under cover of darkness, he heaped box upon box of pyrotechnics, loot thought useless and all but forgotten, in front of the town hall. A drizzle of gasoline for good measure and the flick of a match was all it took.

He barely made it back to the truck when cracks, whirrs and booms ignited the night, aburst with kaleidoscopic neon color spraying every which way in a continuous barrage.

It wasn't long until police flooded the square, busy dispersing droves of curious onlookers who had disregarded curfew, perhaps assuming this most irregular disruption to be some sort of government sanctioned event.

Joseph and the others gathered at the appointed place, numbering about thirty souls.

The silent caravan of only a few packed vehicles filed out of town unnoticed.

They stopped on a plateau at the base going back up into the Sierra, where Maddox's uncle had brought Miriam to wait for them. Words of relief and gratitude were exchanged between the exiles and their helpers.

"I told you it would work, your people can't resist mindless distraction," Mad told Joseph, beaming broadly.

"Not *my* people."

"Stop by to tell me more about your Holy Book sometime."

They embraced before Maddox and Winston went their way.

Joseph leaned on his rifle for alpenstock with Miriam by his side, as a storm, infuriate stygian portent, gravid with fearful lightning, gathered over Repentance in the distance behind them.

The sun rose on the morning when the pastor's voice resounded with gladness, reflected in all present, "I baptize you in the name of the Father, the Son and the Holy Spirit."

The old was buried when Joseph emerged from the pristine, icy water of the glacier lake.

“You are hereby anointed king, priest and prophet in the service of our Lord.” Moser made the sign of the cross on the brow of the reborn with oil.

Over time the assembly of added campers, trailers and wooden structures became an organism of peaceable accord. Miriam’s parents and siblings had joined them.

There was an abundance of fertile soil on which fruits and vegetables grew well. The brooks and springs were crowded with fish, the woods lively with game. A variety of skill and knowledge between them enabled the congregation to serve and edify one another in worshipful gratitude for the blessing of the Almighty.

Miriam wore a light white dress on the wedding day, her hair adorned with delicate wildflowers, lovely with angelic grace, gentle, calm, wholeheartedly surrendered to her Creator and the man He had chosen for her.

Joseph beheld his helpmeet, soothed in soft, untold delight. He knew it was his to aspire to merit her trustful affection, to become worthy of the beauty of her profound love of virtue, her sincere devotion to truth, to what is good, what is just. To God. He felt at that moment an insurmountable sense of bliss at the chance he was then given, to use the rest of his life to do so.

“You have captured my heart, my own, my bride, with one glance of your eyes,” Joseph whispered as he held her hands in his.

“For love burns like a blazing fire, like a mighty flame,” Miriam returned.

When Pastor Moser had performed the rites, they stood united in the bond of holy matrimony.

Celebrating in the trusted and intimate circle of those who now made up their family, there was a fiddle and a guitar, a tambourine and the mingled melody of cheerful voices that reached into the night.

Soon Miriam's belly bulged with reverent anticipation. On mild evenings they climbed up the small ladder onto the roof of their camper, where she would lay her head on her husband's chest, his arms closed around her while the superlunary dome sheltered them in cosmic splendor.

As for the world, Joseph recognized its season. He knew the time at hand would be marked by tribulation yet unimaginable for all who were in and of it. He also knew that his was a hope which eclipsed and eluded such cares. It was Christ and the knowledge of Him that gave life. Indomitable, uncompromised, unending. These things he considered as he addressed God in silence.

Now I understand, by Your grace, the treachery of all, including myself, who have, not for lack of evidence, but for the shunning of Your light, denied in their hearts that which may be openly observed and determined as true, even You... the cornerstone rejected, under which all iniquity, shameless theft of Your creation's joy, must be ground to dust. You alone know what it means to me that You, who are eternal truth and righteousness, will insist with omnipotent majesty on absolute victory. My troubled soul, once beset by my own and all the world's wickedness, now rests safely in Your mighty, merciful hands. Blessed Lord, who are the Image, the Word and the Son of the Father, the Messiah in Glory... how can I express my relief, my gratitude, that You have opened the pages of Your testaments, allowing me not to blaspheme in the imagination of who You might be, but, by Your Holy Spirit, to walk upright in the confidence of who You are. You, who have given Yourself for my redemption while I was yet unworthy. My God, my Maker, my Father, my King, my Savior, my Friend, my Lord... You have freed me from death, cleansed me from filth, established me as heir in Your eternal kingdom, forever and evermore... Christ Jesus, I am Yours.

I, the author of this story, hereby confess
that Jesus Christ is the living God,
Lord and King of my life, that He died on
the cross for the sins of the world and
rose on the third day, soon to return
so that all who repent and believe on Him
will be saved from the wrath to come,
into eternal life.

To share this book with someone for free
please go to:

www.westofrepentance.com

For questions, comments and inquiries contact:

ministry@westofrepentance.com

Printed in Poland
by Amazon Fulfillment
Poland Sp. z o.o., Wrocław

93454938R00120